KIDS CAN'T STOP READING
THE CHOOSE YOUR
OWN ADVENTURE® STORIES!

"Choose Your Own Adventure is the best thing that has come along since books themselves.

_____ 11

"I didn't read _____ my Choose Your O_____ ry night."

——————————————————————————————Chris Brogan, age 13

"I love the control I have over what happens next."
                                    —Kosta Efstathiou, age 17

"Choose Your Own Adventure books are so much fun to read and collect—I want them all!"
                                    —Brendan Davin, age 11

And teachers like this series, too:

"We have read and reread, worn thin, loved, loaned, bought for others, and donated to school libraries our Choose Your Own Adventure books."

CHOOSE YOUR OWN ADVENTURE®—
AND MAKE READING MORE FUN!

Bantam Books in the Choose Your Own Adventure® series
Ask your bookseller for the books you have missed

THE YOUNG INDIANA JONES CHRONICLES™

WHO ARE YOU?

BY EDWARD PACKARD

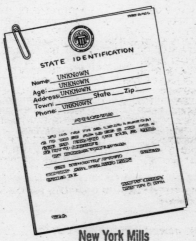

STATE IDENTIFICATION

Name: UNKNOWN
Age: UNKNOWN
Address: UNKNOWN
Town: _____ State ____ Zip ____
Phone: UNKNOWN

ILLUSTRATED BY FRANK BOLLE

BANTAM BOOKS
NEW YORK · TORONTO · LONDON · SYDNEY · AUCKLAND

RL4, age 10 and up

WHO ARE YOU?

A Bantam Book/August 1994

CHOOSE YOUR OWN ADVENTURE® *is a registered*
trademark of Bantam Books,
a division of Bantam Doubleday Dell Publishing Group, Inc.
Registered in U.S. Patent and Trademark Office and elsewhere.

Original conception of Edward Packard

Cover art by Bill Schmidt
Interior illustrations by Frank Bolle

ISBN 0-553-56398-X

Published simultaneously in the United States and Canada

Bantam Books are published by Bantam Books, a division of
Bantam Doubleday Dell Publishing Group, Inc. Its trademark,
consisting of the words "Bantam Books" and the portrayal of a
rooster, is Registered in U.S. Patent and Trademark Office and
in other countries. Marca Registrada. Bantam Books, 1540
Broadway, New York, New York 10036.

PRINTED IN THE UNITED STATES OF AMERICA

OPM   0 9 8 7 6 5 4 3 2 1

WHO
ARE YOU?

WARNING!!!

Do not read this book straight through from beginning to end. These pages contain many different adventures that you may have when you wake up lying in a ditch with no identification, no memory, and no idea of who you are.

From time to time as you read along, you'll have a chance to make a choice. When you've done so, follow the directions to find out what happens to you next.

To discover who you are, you'll have to journey to exciting cities, escape a psychopathic killer, and choose new friends from a world full of strangers. Your survival—and the chance to see your family again—will depend on your quick thinking and good judgment.

Good luck!

You're lying in a ditch alongside a highway. You've got a bump on the head. It hurts. You feel dizzy, and when you try to stand up, you almost fall over. You sit down again and brush little clumps of dirt and grass off your clothes. The sun is shining. The smell of fresh grass and flowers fills the air, but so do the fumes from traffic roaring by on the highway.

Your head is clearing now—you must have just woken up. Suddenly you wonder, *what am I doing here?* Then you have an even scarier thought: *who am I?*

You panic, trying to remember something about yourself. Anything! But all you can think of is something about visiting Uncle Norman. Norman who? Where? You don't know what your name is, or who your parents are. Or what state you're in, or even what country!

One thing you do know is that you're hungry and thirsty. You struggle to your feet and walk a few steps. At least you're alive and don't seem to have any broken bones. You take a few more steps along the ditch. You think to search your pockets for a wallet or some sort of identification. But you find nothing—not a single clue as to who you are.

You feel like crying, but that won't do any good. You climb onto the shoulder of the road, then flinch as a huge tractor-trailer whizzes by. A pickup truck follows. The driver glances at you, probably wondering what you're doing there.

Turn to page 2.

2

The driver of the pickup slows a little, but he's already past you. No chance he'll stop now. You face the traffic and stick out your thumb.

Dozens of cars and trucks go by. Then a delivery truck pulls to a stop on the grass ahead of you. A thin man in a plaid shirt reaches across and opens the passenger door.

He's chewing on a toothpick and is too lazy to take it out while he's talking, so you can't quite make out what he's saying. But it sounds like "Want a ride, kid?" You hop in and pull the door shut behind you.

He starts up and edges back onto the highway. "How far ya going?"

"I don't know," you say. "I got hit in the head, and I can't remember anything, even who I am."

"Whaa?" He looks at you curiously for so long that you're afraid he'll run off the road. Then, shaking his head, he says, "Well, you must belong to someone around here. I'll take you to the sheriff. First I've got to make a delivery. It will only take a minute—this exit coming up here."

A moment later he turns onto the ramp.

"I don't even know where we are," you say.

"Ward's Corner, Missouri," the driver says. "Population seven hundred and eighty-three, not including the chickens." He laughs, but right now you're not finding anything very funny. You're in a state of shock from realizing that you don't know who you are.

_____

Go on to the next page.

The deliveryman drives past a gas station and a farm stand, turns up a street lined with pasture land, then pulls into a long driveway. The sign at the entrance says CRUSOE.

At the end of the drive is a white farmhouse with a broad, sloping lawn shaded by old maple trees. Set off to the side further back is a freshly painted red barn. A big black dog races around from behind it, barking and wagging its tail.

A moment later you notice a huge bird, like a prehistoric monster, flapping its wings between two trees to one side of the house. You quickly see that it's made of wood, and that the wind is making its wings flap. Then you notice another bird, not as big but with a great beak and glittering eyes. The sight makes you smile.

The driver stops. "I'll just be a minute." He gets out, opens the door at the back of the truck, and pulls out a package. As he starts toward the house, a man and a woman come out to meet him. He hands over the package; then the three of them get in a long conversation. You feel like stretching, so you jump out of the truck.

The man and woman look at you strangely, then go off by themselves, as if they don't want the deliveryman to hear them. You wonder what's going on.

The dog comes up to you, still wagging its tail, acting as if it would like to play. You pat it awhile, then look over to see what's keeping the driver. He's talking with the man and woman again.

Turn to page 94.

4

"I'll meet the Shermans," you say.

As Mr. Conklin predicted, the Shermans take a liking to you. They tell you that they really want to be your foster parents. But you're not sure you like them that much. Mr. Sherman is a big, fleshy man with a broad grin. He gestures frantically as he talks. It makes you nervous. Mrs. Sherman, who is rather overweight, carries on a mile a minute about how you'll like living in Beverly Hills, which is where their home is. They tell you they have a daughter named Alicia who is about your age. They didn't bring her along, however, so you'll just have to hope she's okay.

The next day you arrive in Beverly Hills, California, home to many famous movie stars. The Shermans' house is practically a palace, a big granite structure with marble columns, a huge front hall, and more rooms than you can keep track of. In the back is a terrace you could fit hundreds of people on. At the far edge is a large swimming pool shaped to look like a natural pond. Beyond is a miniature cliff with a waterfall that flows into the pool. High hedges and evergreens screen off the neighbors' yards.

While the Shermans are showing you the pool, their daughter saunters out onto the terrace. Alicia, like her mother, is a bit tubby.

Go on to the next page.

"Alicia, darling," Mrs. Sherman calls. "Come meet your foster sibling." She turns to you. "Oh, dear, we don't know what your name is." She lets out a little laugh. "And you don't either."

"How about Lee?" Mr. Sherman says. "Lee Terrell. I can see that name on the marquee of a movie theater."

Turn to page 34.

6

You stay in the cart. Nothing happens for a few minutes. Then, just as you're thinking of giving up and getting out, the cart starts moving. The nightmares start moving too: lights come on. A *Tyrannosaurus rex* leaps out from behind a cliff. It lunges at you. You shrink back, but of course it can't get you.

As soon as your cart passes this nightmare, a twelve-foot-high robot bears down on you. His hands are heavy steel pincers that open and shut as he walks. Your cart is headed right at him.

You scream. The cart doesn't stop, but at the last moment it veers away, keeping you out of the robot's grip. Then you're thrown back in your seat as the cart speeds up, so fast you're afraid it's going out of control. You tear around a curve. Ahead is a waterfall. You're going to crash into it. You *do* crash into it, but somehow you don't get wet. The "water" falling is just a hologram. You hear screams—something's happening to the people in the cart ahead of you. Then you remember there isn't any cart ahead of you. The next moment you're blinded by brilliant sunlight. You're out of the cave. But your nightmare isn't over. Your cart has stopped in front of the security guard and two policemen.

You don't know who you are, but right now you wish you were someone else.

The End

You feel like wringing your hands, or wringing Mr. Conklin's neck! Wherever you go, you can't seem to find anyone to help you.

After the interview is finished, Mr. Conklin turns you over to the day proctor, Ms. Weaver, who shows you the bunk room where you'll be sleeping. She assigns you a cot and a small chest of drawers. She also gives you some extra clothing, since you have nothing but the jeans, shirt, and jacket you were wearing when you woke up in the ditch.

You feel kind of dazed and put the clothing in the drawers without even checking to see if it fits. Ms. Weaver tells you to get some rest and to check with her if you have any problems. She's about to leave when some other kids come through the door. They've been at instructional classes, she explains.

Ms. Weaver introduces you to the kids sharing your bunk room, and you meet the others at dinner in the cafeteria. Counting you, there are thirty-five children at the shelter—twenty boys who sleep in one of two bunk rooms and fifteen girls who sleep in one of two others.

In the days ahead you learn that life is very monotonous at the children's shelter. You get up at seven in the morning, make your bed, eat breakfast, and then either have to wash the dishes, mop the floors, or clean up the bathrooms. Then you go to "instructional classes," which are sort of like school, except there is no real attempt to teach you much.

Turn to page 92.

You explain how you found yourself in the ditch and haven't been able to remember anything before then. The sheriff listens without the slightest expression on his face.

When you're finished, he says, "It sounds like you got some kind of brain damage, unless you're just making this up."

"I'm *not*," you say, annoyed.

" 'Cause if you didn't have brain damage, I'd have to charge you with vagrancy," he says in a grave tone.

Meanwhile you're thinking that the deliveryman was right. Sheriff Dagney is a blockhead.

"As it is," he continues, "I think I'd better take you to the nearest hospital. It's in Blakemore, about twenty miles from here."

"But my family may be looking for me," you say.

"I'm in charge," Dagney says sharply. "And I say you should go to the hospital." He puts some papers in his desk drawer and takes out a set of keys. "Okay, kid, let's go." He locks up the office and leads you out to his car. You get in the front seat with him, casting your eyes at the shotgun mounted above the windshield.

The sheriff drives up the street and then onto the interstate. He turns on the radio. You assume he's tuning in to the police channel. Instead it's a country-and-western music station.

After you've both listened to twenty minutes of heartbreak songs and commercials, he turns off at an exit marked BLAKEMORE.

Turn to page 43.

You lie down and try to rest, but you feel like jumping up and running off someplace. You don't need rest. You need to find your family!

Finally you doze off. You're awakened by two men and a woman who say that they are specialists and listen while you tell your story. Then they attach electrodes to your head and hook you up to a machine that measures your brain waves. They ask questions to see if you can think straight and remember things like who the president is and what day of the week comes after Monday.

Turn to page 79.

12

"At least you aren't missing school, since it's the middle of July," Mrs. Crusoe says.

When you hear that, you give a little start.

"What's the matter, dear?" Mrs. Crusoe says, touching your shoulder.

"Nothing," you say. "It's just that I didn't even know what month it was, only that it was summertime."

"Well it's July twelfth," Mr. Crusoe says. "So you can start counting from there."

"Hey Dad!" Damon practically jumps out of his chair. "Don't forget, you promised we could go to Daredevil Park."

"Daredevil Park? What's that?" you ask.

"It's the wildest amusement park in the country," Mr. Crusoe says. "Damon's talking about the new branch they opened recently, about a two-hour drive from here."

"When are we going?" Damon taps the table with excitement.

"When I get a break in my work," Mr. Crusoe says. "I told you sometime this summer, and I meant it."

Turn to page 78.

You lean back in the booth to think, as Lars pays the check. Hiring a private detective sounds like a good idea. Detectives uncover clues and track down missing persons all the time. Then again, you haven't had much luck with investigators so far. Maybe you should try something different. Like visiting the hypnotist.

"So what are you going to do?" Cheetah asks as you get up from the table.

If you decide to hire a private detective, turn to page 45.

If you decide to go to the hypnotist, turn to page 88.

"It's true I'd like to get out of here, Mr. Conklin," you say. "But I couldn't be happy being the child of someone besides my own parents."

"Have it your way," the director says, shaking his head. "I think you're missing a great opportunity."

You leave his office feeling that you made the right decision but also thinking about how long you may be stuck in the children's shelter.

Months pass. Kids come and go, some nice, some not so nice, some practically criminals. You learn how to handle them all, and the proctors and Mr. Conklin too. Still, the shelter isn't much fun. You go to classes every day, but you guess you must be missing a lot by not being in your own school.

Turn to page 25.

You, Cheetah, and Lars have a simple breakfast of muffins and orange juice. Lars makes some phone calls and comes up with the name of a detective: Henry Whitaker. He makes an appointment for you to see Mr. Whitaker later that morning and takes you over there in his minivan. Cheetah comes along to keep you company.

When you arrive, Mr. Whitaker's secretary asks you to wait in the reception room. After about twenty minutes she leads you into his office.

Whitaker is an overweight, balding man, not exactly a James Bond type, but he has sharp blue eyes and a confident manner that gives you the feeling he knows what he's doing. You sit down across from his desk. A sign on it says, WE CAN DO IT!

Again you tell your story, including why you haven't talked to the police.

Turn to page 66.

16

Dr. Wolsey pulls out a round silver watch and dangles it on a string in front of your eyes. You can hear it ticking. He begins swinging it gently. It shimmers as the light strikes it from different angles.

"Keep your eye on the watch," he says, speaking in a slow, monotonous voice. "You are fascinated by how the light changes on the watch, changes as it swings and swings in the changing light. Changing with the swings, back and forth, back and forth, back and forth, swinging in the light. You are slowly getting sleepy as it swings and swings and swings, sleepier as it swings until now you are asleep."

At that moment you feel asleep and yet still somehow awake.

"Think back to when you were visiting your uncle Norman," Dr. Wolsey says. "Were you having a nice time there?"

"Yes," you say.

"And why were you having a nice time? What were you doing?"

"My cousin and I went horseback riding, and we went river-rafting."

"And your cousin's name is?"

"Charlie."

"Charlie and you were having fun, but then something happened that wasn't fun. What was that?"

You suddenly feel upset.

"It was not fun at all," Dr. Wolsey says in a sharper voice. "What was it that happened?"

Turn to page 28.

18

You duck into the tunnel and dash past a line of carts set on a track that runs through the exhibit. You crouch down in front of the first cart to catch your breath, hoping the security guard won't come after you.

Ahead of you is a cavern, shrouded in darkness. You walk a few steps along the track, trying to see if there might be another exit. You see an electric panel control box a few feet away. This must be where the attendant sends each cart on its way. You step over and look at it. There's a green START button and a red STOP button. You push the green button, then race back and jump in the lead cart. It starts moving, taking you into the Cave of Nightmares.

Except there are no nightmares now. The rest of the exhibit hasn't been turned on yet. There isn't any light. You roll along in utter darkness, wondering where you're going.

Go on to the next page.

Suddenly the cart stops. Someone has turned off the power. You sit there a minute, half-expecting security guards with flashlights to come looking for you.

But they don't. That's a relief. Still, you don't want to stay in the cart all day. You must decide how to get out of the cave.

If you wait in the cart for a while, turn to page 6.

If you get out and walk back along the track, turn to page 69.

If you get out and walk forward along the track, turn to page 26.

You tell Cheetah you're game to try the escape.

The night before the fire drill you go to bed with your clothes on. It takes you a long time to get to sleep. You seem to have just dozed off when the clanging alarm bell jars you to consciousness. For a few seconds you can't imagine what's going on. Then, remembering, you're out of your bunk in a flash.

Cheetah is already waiting for you in the hall. "Let's go," he says.

The bunk rooms open onto a long corridor that runs the length of the building. There are two doors, one near the bunk rooms and another at the far end of the hall. You and Cheetah race down to the far end. In the dim hall light you read the sign on the door.

EMERGENCY EXIT ONLY—FIRE ALARM WILL
SOUND IF LATCH PULLED. SEVERE PENALTY
FOR UNAUTHORIZED USE.

No need to worry about that: the fire alarm is already sounding!

Go on to the next page.

Cheetah takes a last look back down the hall, then pulls on the latch. The door won't open.

"It's still locked," he wails.

You grab the latch and try yourself. No luck.

Cheetah looks stunned. "It's supposed to open if the fire alarm goes off. That's the law!" Again he rattles the latch, but the door stays locked tight. Meanwhile all the other kids are piling out of the bunk rooms, some only half dressed.

Turn to page 108.

You decide to learn about astrology from Mrs. Crusoe. The next morning Mrs. Crusoe sets out some charts showing the planets, the moon, and the sun and how they move in relation to the stars.

"The celestial bodies are in a certain position at the moment of each person's birth," she says. "The pattern of these bodies at the time of your birth affects your whole life. By studying them an astrologer can guide you so that you can better plan your activities. Important events are also affected by the stars. Astrologers can tell you when conditions are favorable or unfavorable for a particular event."

"Have you really helped people this way?" you ask.

Mrs. Crusoe adjusts her position, sitting up stiffly in her chair. "I really think I have. People often tell me how much help I've been."

"I guess you can't help me, though," you say. "I don't know the date I was born."

Mrs. Crusoe scowls. She consults her charts for a few moments. "It's true I've never had that problem before," she says. Then her face brightens. "I know—the key date is not the date of your birth but the day you were born to us!"

"I wasn't born to you," you say firmly.

She flashes a smile. "Born in the sense you came to us—on July twelfth." Turning back to her charts, she says, "Let me see . . . July twelfth . . ."

"Do you really believe all this?" you ask.

Turn to page 89.

In a couple of days you're back in your own home. It's wonderful to be there, with your real family, and with your memory restored.

"We missed you so much, and we were terribly worried about you," your mom says. "But somehow I knew you'd be all right."

"Those people were sick," your dad says. "The way they pretended to be looking for your family."

The next day you learn that Mr. and Mrs. Crusoe have been charged with kidnapping and several other crimes. A few weeks later you're required to come to court to testify at the trial. The Crusoes' defense is that they didn't really kidnap you, that you were never restrained and were free to leave anytime you wanted. Their lawyer points out that they didn't abuse you. They treated you like their own child. The prosecutor argues that their crime was in lying to you, pretending they were trying to locate your family when they weren't.

In view of the facts, the jury doesn't find the Crusoes guilty of kidnapping, but they find them guilty of several lesser crimes. The judge decides not to send them to jail but requires them to get psychiatric counseling. He also sentences them to a year's probation and two years' community service.

Turn to page 30.

One day about ten weeks after you have decided not to become a foster child, a group of visitors arrives at the shelter. Their leader is a middle-aged African-American woman with a stern look on her face. The visitors tour all the halls and rooms, even the bathrooms. Mr. Conklin and a couple of staff proctors tag along. You can tell these aren't ordinary visitors by how nervous Mr. Conklin acts with them.

Later that day news spreads like wildfire: the visitors are from the State Department of Welfare, and they have found Mr. Conklin guilty of all sorts of lapses in managing the shelter. He's in big trouble.

Soon afterward, a proctor comes looking for you in your bunk room. With him is the woman who was leading the visitors. She strides up to you and shakes your hand.

Turn to page 99.

26

You walk forward along the track, hoping to find another way out. You've been walking for about a minute when lights come on. The ride must have started up.

You round a sharp bend. A giant robot is standing just off the track. Its hands are steel pincers, ready to crush any human-sized prey.

People are screaming. You look and see the lead cart coming, rounding the bend at high speed. You jump sideways in time to keep from being hit but land right in the path of the giant robot! The cart races by, the two boys in it screaming at the top of their lungs. They are out of reach of the robot's awesome grip. Unfortunately, you're not.

The End

"I had gone down the road from Uncle Norman's house to the general store. I was walking back and a van pulled up to a stop. I thought it was someone who wanted to ask directions, but then two men jumped out. They grabbed me and locked me in the back of the van."

"Did they say anything?"

"They said, 'You're the Moncrieff kid, aren't you? We've been looking for you!'"

"And is your name Moncrieff?" Dr. Wolsey asks.

"No," you say, and suddenly you blurt out your real name!

Dr. Wolsey's eyebrows go up. "Ah," he exclaims. "A breakthrough."

"My name's not Moncrieff," you repeat. "I told them I never heard of anyone named Moncrieff."

"And they didn't believe you?"

"They just wouldn't." Thinking about that horrible moment, when the men took you out of the van and questioned you, you almost burst into tears.

"That's all right," Dr. Wolsey says. "You'll be all right. They mistook you for a child named Moncrieff. You have never heard that name, but *I* have. It's a very rich family. It's obvious they thought they were kidnapping the Moncrieff child, and when they found out they had seized someone else, they threw you into the ditch."

Go on to the next page.

"They said they had wasted their time on me," you say.

"They had wasted *your* time," Dr. Wolsey says. "Now when I clap my hands three times you are going to wake up. Ready?"

"Ready," you say.

You hear a *CLAP!* And suddenly you're awake—remembering nothing about what you just told Dr. Wolsey, but everything else you had forgotten!

Turn to page 47.

After the trial, you say good-bye to Mr. and Mrs. Crusoe and to Damon. You tell them that you forgive them for not being honest with you, and that you wish them well.

At first, your mom and dad tell you that they will never forgive the Crusoes. But when you put up the beautiful flapping bird that Mr. Crusoe taught you to make they say that they may forgive the Crusoes after all.

The End

"I think so," you say.

"Then it would be easy to reach a branch you could climb out on and drop down outside the fence. We could be out of here before anyone noticed."

"This sounds a little tricky," you say.

"It's not so tricky, but we have to be careful. They warned us that if anyone tried to run away they'd be sent to the reformatory." Cheetah glances nervously down the hall. "How much money you got?"

"About seven bucks."

"I got sixteen. Plenty. We'll have to hurry into town once we're out. That way we can be on the six *a.m.* bus to Center City before anyone figures out we're missing." Cheetah sounds very sure of himself, but you're getting the jitters.

"So, are you game?" he asks.

You're as eager as Cheetah to get out of the children's shelter, but you don't like the risk of being sent to the reformatory. You could be trapped there for years with some of the toughest, meanest kids in the state. "I'll think about it overnight," you tell him.

*If you decide to try to escape,
turn to page 20.*

*If you decide not to risk it,
turn to page 72.*

There's plenty of room in the cab for the two of you, but the driver doesn't invite you to get in.

"Where are you kids going?" he says.

"Chicago," says Cheetah.

The driver gives you a long look. "So am I, but you better have a good reason for going there, or I'll have to give the cops a call on my radio."

"We do have a good reason," Cheetah says. "We're going to visit my brother."

The driver looks you both over again. He scowls, and his lips tighten. "Had a bad time at home?" he says.

"Uh-huh," Cheetah says.

"So did I," the driver says. "Come on in."

He opens the passenger door. You and Cheetah climb aboard. He puts the truck in gear and starts up the ramp.

Cheetah nudges you, grinning. You don't know what's going to happen, but you feel a thrill of excitement. You're sure this driver won't turn you in. And though you still don't know who you are, and you only have seven cents in your pocket, in some strange way you feel in control of your life: you're on the move, on the road, headed for the big city!

Turn to page 84.

"Wonderful," Mrs. Sherman says, turning to you. "Lee, meet Alicia Sherman."

Alicia comes up, and the two of you awkwardly shake hands. She has a nice smile. You have a feeling you'll probably like her.

Later the Shermans show you your room. It's gigantic. It has a thick rug, windows overlooking the pool, a TV, VCR, and stereo, an intercom phone, bookcases, a huge stuffed giraffe whose head almost scrapes the ceiling, and your own walk-in closet, which seems especially weird since you have only a few articles of clothing.

When you go to bed that night you're amazed at how big the bed is, and how comfortable, and how many pillows you have. Still, you'd rather be in your own bed, even though you don't know what it's like or where it is.

The next morning breakfast is served in the "atrium," a room that has a glass wall and ceiling and is half full of flowering plants. Sun streams through the windows. Music plays through speakers hung on the walls. A maid serves the food, asking everyone what they would like, as if you were at a restaurant.

As you sit down, Mrs. Sherman keeps her eyes on you a long time. Finally, embarrassed, you meet her gaze.

"Lee, darling," she says, "you're perfect."

"Perfect?"

"For a role in the movie I'm casting!"

Turn to page 57.

The fire chief yells something to the men uncoiling the hose. They start reeling it up again.

"I guess the drill is over," Cheetah says. "Looks like we're stuck here."

Suddenly you have an inspiration. You grab Cheetah's arm. "I think we can turn the tables on Mr. Conklin. Come on."

You run up to where the director is talking to the fire chief. Cheetah follows.

"Get back with the others, you two," Conklin yells.

You pay no attention but turn to the chief. "Chief, you should know that the fire door wouldn't open at the other end of the building."

"Did you hear me?" Mr. Conklin snaps at you.

"Just a minute," the fire chief says in an even sharper tone. "I want to hear about this!"

You tell how you and Cheetah were almost crushed against the door by kids trying to get out.

"This sounds like a serious violation of the fire code," the chief says to Conklin. "Let's you and I inspect that door right now." He takes hold of Conklin's elbow and starts leading him back toward the building.

Cheetah whispers, "Let's go."

The two of you slip past the other firemen and some onlookers, right through the open gate. You dart behind a fire engine and then take off down the street.

Turn to page 105.

He looks at you strangely for a moment, as if wondering if you can be trusted. Then he says, "I've been looking for someone to make a break with me. You interested?"

"I'd think about it," you say. "But how? The doors are locked and the windows are barred."

"The doors at each end of the hall unlock automatically if the fire alarm goes off," he says in a low voice. "They're supposed to have drills every once in a while, but they haven't had one for as long as anyone can remember." Cheetah begins smirking—you can tell he has something up his sleeve. "They made me come in to see the director the other day," he goes on. "While I was waiting by his desk I saw a letter to him from the fire commissioner *ordering* him to have a fire drill next Wednesday morning at five *a.m.* He said he was going to have a station house drill at the same time—with trucks coming and everything to make it realistic."

"So we're going to get wakened up even earlier than usual."

Cheetah moves closer, his dark eyes flashing. "We'll *want* to wake up. When the alarm goes off, the door near the kitchen, the one that's never used, will unlock automatically. We can walk right out."

"We'd still have to get over the fence around the property," you say.

"From that door we can get to a tree that's up against the fence," says Cheetah. "Can you shinny up a tree for about six feet?"

Turn to page 31.

"We're going to take you to the hospital and check you out," the medic says. "I think you're going to be just fine."

You would think so too if you could figure out what happened to your memory. There's a big gap in it!

As they are putting you on a stretcher, two officers come up. One of them starts questioning you, but the other interrupts.

"Hey, this is one of the kidnap victims. I remember seeing the picture."

"You're right!" the other exclaims. "Get on the phone and report this."

A moment later the medics carry you to the ambulance and load you in. The ambulance starts up. The siren comes on. You're on your way to the hospital. When you arrive there, your parents are already on the phone, eager to speak to you. Up until now they had no idea where you were.

Turn to page 117.

"I'm truly sorry we didn't," Mr. Crusoe says.

"And I feel the same way," says his wife. "When I saw Damon dangling up there, I knew what it must be like to lose a child. Then I realized how wrong we had been in not notifying anyone that we had found a missing person."

"You also realized how silly astrology is," Mr. Crusoe says.

Despite the Crusoes' apologies, the police ask you if you want to press charges against them.

"No," you say. "I don't want them to go to jail. I'd rather give them a chance to be the good people I know they are."

The End

"I think I'd better go to the sheriff," you say.

"Of course it's up to you," the man says.

"We're sorry you're not staying," the woman says. Even the dog looks a little sad.

You wave good-bye and hop up into the truck. The driver takes you into town. Ward's Corner isn't much more than a gas station, convenience store, post office, shopping plaza, and a miniature village green. Across from the green is a small, white-framed building with the words CITY HALL over the door. A door to one side says SHERIFF.

The deliveryman parks and escorts you inside. A gray-haired man with a paunch and a grizzled face is sitting with his feet up on his desk reading a newspaper. A sign on the desk says W. T. DAGNEY, SHERIFF.

"I found this kid by the side of the road," the deliveryman says. "Seems to have amnesia or something."

The sheriff squints at you as if there were a bright light, which there isn't.

"Excuse me, I'm way behind schedule," the deliveryman says. He turns to leave.

"Thanks," you say.

He half-waves at you without turning around. "Good luck, kid."

"So what happened to you?" the sheriff asks.

Turn to page 9.

Damon runs off and quickly returns with a couple of oversize towels. "Come on," he says, and starts up the staircase. You follow, with the dog cutting in ahead of you.

"Hannibal, it's dinnertime," Mrs. Crusoe calls from below.

At the word "dinner," the dog practically does a flip and races back downstairs.

Damon shows you your bedroom. You thought it would be a guest room, but it's made up like a kid's room—with posters, stuffed animals, a bookcase filled with children's books and games, and a large bird-kite hung up on the wall.

"Do you have a brother or sister?" you ask Damon.

He looks down at his shoes. "I was supposed to. This was going to be its room but Mom wasn't able to have another."

Turn to page 60.

A few minutes later, the sheriff pulls up to the Blakemore Hospital emergency entrance and checks you in.

A young doctor comes out and takes a look at you. He peers into your eyes at close range and then touches the bump on your head, which has gotten a lot smaller since you regained consciousness in the ditch. The doctor talks a little with the sheriff off to one side.

The sheriff nods, then comes over to you and says, "You're in good hands." He walks off before you even think to ask him if he's going to check with the state police about you.

The doctor leads you into a small room. It has white walls and a padded table with a cloth covering it. "Take your sneakers off and lie down and rest," he says. "The neurologist will be in to examine you soon."

"Could you call the state police and see if they're looking for me?" you say.

He looks at you curiously. "I'm sure the sheriff must have done that." He closes the door behind him.

Turn to page 11.

"I think I'll try a private detective," you say.

Lars and Cheetah nod. "We'll find one in the morning," Lars says. "I'm beat."

So are you. That night you sleep on the foam pad on the floor of Lars's studio. The walls around you are covered with huge paintings of strange, colorful shapes that remind you of rocks and parts of trees, insects and birds. The details are finely done. The more you look at them, the more you see. You wonder who buys the paintings and how much Lars gets paid for them.

When you wake up in the morning the paintings startle you until you remember where you are. This is where Lars works. You realize that you can't stay here long.

Turn to page 15.

46

True to her word, Mrs. Crusoe lets you listen in while she calls the state police. She leaves you alone while she goes to tell Mr. Crusoe what's happening.

A patrol car arrives an hour later. Mr. and Mrs. Crusoe go out to meet them. Meanwhile, you've been waiting, thinking. You're still mad that the Crusoes didn't call the police when they said they would. Yet they've been so nice to you that you don't want them to get in trouble.

A few moments later two policemen come in. They ask you to tell them everything you remember. It doesn't take long—barely twenty-four hours have passed since you woke up in the ditch without any idea of who you were.

While you and the Crusoes wait, one of the officers calls police headquarters to relay the information you have given him. A few minutes later he gets off the phone, grinning.

"I have some good news," he tells you. And does he ever! Your name, the names of all your family members, where you live, everything! Hearing these things wakes up your whole memory. It all comes back—including how you were kidnapped, taken on a three-day ride, first in the back of a panel truck and then in a van, and how you were finally thrown out the door and into a ditch when the kidnappers thought they were going to get caught.

Turn to page 119.

You tell Dr. Wolsey all about yourself.

"Wonderful, wonderful," he says. "I was afraid we might have to have another session or two." He hands you a telephone. "Do you remember your home phone number?"

"I sure do," you say as you start dialing. "I'll never forget it again."

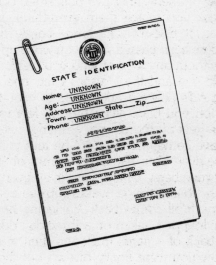

The End

48

You reach for the handle and flick the latch. The driver grabs at you. The car swerves. You get the door open, but a powerful hand grips your arm.

You hear the blaring horn of an oncoming car. The man tries to avoid it while still holding on to you. He loses control. His grip loosens. You leap through the half-open door, landing on the shoulder of the road, and spin forward, twisting, somersaulting, skidding along the grass. You hear the sound of cars crashing before your head hits something hard, knocking you out cold.

Turn to page 68.

50

You wave good-bye to the deliveryman and watch as he pulls out the drive.

Mrs. Crusoe tousles your hair. "We have an extra room you can sleep in tonight," she says, "but right now you need a shower and a shampoo. Damon will show you where to go while Mr. Crusoe and I call the state police and the missing persons bureau."

"We need another towel," Damon says.

"There are a bunch of them in the dryer. Grab a couple on your way upstairs," Mrs. Crusoe says. Turning to you she asks, "You can't remember anything, dear, not even your name?"

You shake your head.

"Do you mind if we call you Evan—temporarily? That's what we were going to name our next child, but it was a blessing that never came."

"Evan?" you repeat. Whatever your real name is, you're pretty sure it's not Evan.

"We just don't want to say, 'Hey you,' " Mr. Crusoe says with a grin.

"It's only temporary," his wife adds. "Okay?"

"I guess so," you answer. It doesn't seem like a good time to argue, and as she says, it's only temporary.

You accompany the Crusoes inside. The house is obviously very old. In fact it almost seems a little slanted, as if one side has settled more than the other. There's a comfortable-looking sofa and chairs in the living room and colorful paintings on the walls.

Turn to page 42.

Fear takes hold of you. But Damon is pointing at something, a helicopter is racing toward you. A minute later it's hovering above you. A harness is lowered. First Damon and then you are pulled up inside. In a few minutes you're safely back on the ground.

Mr. and Mrs. Crusoe break through the crowd. They don't reach you as fast as the news team, however. A man thrusts a microphone in your face while the woman trains her camera on you.

Turn to page 107.

You decide to go to the children's shelter. Soon afterward a van picks you up at the hospital. The driver swings the door open and tells you to get in the back. You climb in and sit down while he gets in the driver's seat. You're startled to see there's a heavy wire grating between the front and rear compartments, the kind police have so that they can take in criminals without being vulnerable to attack.

It's a bad sign, you think, and there's nothing to change your mind when you reach your destination. The children's shelter is a dismal brick building with bars over the windows. A high wrought iron fence surrounds the property.

Turn to page 118.

Lars arrives a half hour later. He's tall and slim with blond hair and doesn't look anything like Cheetah. He seems happy to see his brother, and though he's obviously surprised to find someone with him, he greets you with a smile. He takes you both to a nearby place called the Eatery for dinner.

Lars asks why Cheetah brought you along. You tell him your story.

"I've never met anyone with amnesia," he says. "I sure hope you can get over it."

"Thanks," you say.

"Where are we going to sleep?" Cheetah asks.

"I can put you up on the daybed, little brother," Lars says. Looking at you, he says, "I have a foam rubber pad I use when I go backpacking. You can sleep on that tonight. Tomorrow we'll try to find out who you are."

"That's what I want more than anything in the world," you say. "But how am I going to do it?"

"You might go to a private detective," Lars says after a moment's thought. "A good one should be able to find your family for you. But maybe you could find out even faster if you went to a hypnotist. A friend of mine knows one who's supposed to be amazing."

"A hypnotist? Don't they put people in a trance?"

Go on to the next page.

"You're already in a trance," Cheetah says, poking your arm playfully.

"The hypnotist puts you in a trance," Lars says. "But for a good purpose. He can get you to remember things you couldn't otherwise, things that are buried in your subconscious."

Turn to page 13.

"Wow, are you lucky!" Alicia says. "Mom hasn't found a role for me yet, and she's found one for you the first day you're here!"

You smile, thinking how amazing it is that Mr. Conklin's prediction may actually come true.

It does comes true! A few weeks later you're on a movie lot, acting the role of a kid who is captured during an Indian raid in 1883. You never thought of yourself as much of an actor. But the film has a good director, and you learn fast.

A few months later the film begins appearing in theaters. A close friend of your mother's happens to watch it. In fact she watches it twice just to make sure that it's you she's seeing on the screen. Of course she quickly tells your real parents. After that, it takes them only a couple of days to track you down.

Your parents are overjoyed to find you and bring you home. The Shermans, on the other hand, are sad to have you go.

"Maybe we'll see you again in Hollywood," Mrs. Sherman says.

"I bet we will," Alicia says.

"I know we will," Mr. Sherman says. "Kid, you're going to be a movie star."

The End

58

You tell the Crusoes you'd rather take a day to rest and think about things.

"That's a good idea," Mrs. Crusoe says.

The next day at breakfast Mr. and Mrs. Crusoe are all smiles. "Guess what?" Mr. Crusoe says. "We've decided today would be a good day to go to Daredevil Park!"

"Wow, great!" Damon says.

"Neat," you say, though you're a little confused by how you feel. You'd been planning to run away, but you'd also like to go to Daredevil Park. You could run away from there after you've had some fun, but that doesn't exactly seem fair.

"You don't look too enthusiastic, Evan," Mrs. Crusoe says. "Would you rather not go?"

"Sure, I'd love to," you say without thinking.

Mr. Crusoe gulps down the last of his coffee. "Then let's get ready to leave as soon as possible. It's quite a drive."

After several hours on the interstate, you take the turnoff to Daredevil Park.

"Now don't expect too much," Mr. Crusoe says. "This is a relatively small park and doesn't have all the rides and attractions that made the original Daredevil Park so famous."

"But they have a couple of very scary things," Damon says.

"Indeed," Mrs. Crusoe says. "Daredevil Park is known for its dangerous rides. I wouldn't let you kids risk them, except the astrological signs indicate that today is a completely safe day."

Turn to page 96.

"That's for sure," you answer the director.

"Well then, shall I tell them to come? They have to travel all the way from California, and I'm not going to put them to the trouble and expense unless you say you're willing to go with them."

"Who are these people? Can't I know more about them?"

"Let's see." Mr. Conklin riffles through some papers and pauses to read something. "Mr. Sherman is a movie producer and Mrs. Sherman is a casting agent, someone who finds actors for roles in the movies. They have one other child, but they can't have any more of their own. Of course they have been thoroughly investigated. The welfare agency wouldn't allow anyone to be a foster parent who didn't have a good character and record. I strongly recommend you accept the offer."

"I don't know," you say. "This might make it harder for my real parents to find me."

"It might make it easier," the director says. "You might get a role in a movie, and they would see you in it." He chuckles.

"Sure," you say sarcastically. Still, you're tempted by the offer. Almost anything seems better than staying in the children's shelter.

If you say you'd be willing to have the Shermans be your foster parents, turn to page 4.

If you say you'd rather stay at the shelter, turn to page 14.

You feel like asking why it's fixed up as if the child had actually been born and grown up there, but you decide that wouldn't be polite. You just say it's a nice room and head for the shower.

After you've washed up, Damon lends you some fresh clothes, which fit amazingly well, while Mrs. Crusoe throws your dirty ones in the washer. Then you have a really good dinner, the kind that makes you realize how hungry you were. Unfortunately, as you sit down to eat, Mr. Crusoe breaks the news that the police have no record of anyone missing who fits your description.

"Don't worry, though," he says. "I'm sure they'll find your real family."

Turn to page 12.

"Calm down," Dr. Hestor says sharply. "They are not stupid tests. They are very expensive, and they've been paid for by the state welfare fund. You should be grateful for the care that's been provided."

"Why haven't the police come to talk to me?"

"Perhaps they'll arrange that at the children's shelter. You're in their care now. Their van will be here to pick you up in about half an hour. So get dressed and be ready, all right?"

"Okay," you say.

Dr. Hestor smiles for the first time. "Good luck to you," she says, and then she's gone.

You sit dejectedly on the edge of your bed. The idea of going to the children's shelter is depressing. Maybe you should take off on your own. You only have seven dollars in your pocket, but you could probably hitchhike out of town. The trouble is, if you get caught, you might be worse off than at the shelter.

If you decide to take your chances at the children's shelter, turn to page 53.

If you decide to try to get out of town, turn to page 87.

You spot a sign up ahead: WHITLEY, NEXT EXIT.

The driver pulls over to the right lane and slows. A truck is coming up close behind you. You lean over the backseat and wave frantically, trying to get the truck driver's attention. But at that moment the man driving you veers suddenly onto the exit ramp. The truck barrels past.

You've lost that chance, but a few hundred yards ahead is a stop sign. That should be a good time to get out.

The driver slows a little, but instead of stopping, he accelerates, almost putting the car in a spin as it screeches around the corner and onto another road.

"You should have stopped there," you say angrily.

He laughs and guns the engine. It would be insane to dive out of the car now.

He rounds a sharp curve. A truck is ahead of him and he can't pass it because of a car coming from the opposite direction. You glance at the speedometer. It drops to thirty miles an hour, then twenty-five, then twenty as the oncoming car whizzes by. Now that he can pass the truck he'll speed up. This may be your last chance to escape. But you may not survive the fall.

*If you open the door and bail out,
turn to page 48.*

*If you decide to wait for a safer chance,
turn to page 106.*

64

A crowd is gathering around the base of the wheel. Attendants are trying to keep people back.

A gust of wind hits you, setting your car swinging and twisting the thin cable that's keeping you from plunging to the ground.

You exchange glances with Damon, who is white with fear.

Below you a van screeches to a stop. Newspeople jump out. A woman aims a video camera up at you.

If we fall, they'll have the action on TV, you think.

A siren sounds as a fire truck arrives. The firemen raise a ladder from the truck, but it's nowhere near high enough to reach you. They start bringing down people seated in the lower cars. Another gust of wind sends your car spinning, tightening the cable even more.

You scream down, *"Can't you crank the wheel around?"*

"No!" the answer comes back. *"It would put too much strain on the cable."*

Turn to page 51.

66

"This is an unusual situation," Whitaker says. "Quite often someone comes in and wants me to find a missing person. But in your case a missing person comes in and wants me to find someone else—namely your parents. Normally, I would know the name of the person I'm looking for. But *you* can't remember the names of your parents, or of anyone else for that matter!"

"Except that I have an uncle named Norman," you say. "I was visiting him before this happened."

"What kind of a man was your uncle Norman? Was he the sort that might treat you badly?"

"I don't think so," you say. "But I don't know. I can't remember anything but his first name."

"Hmm. That's a pretty weak clue."

"Maybe so," you say, pointing to the sign on his desk. "But remember your motto—*we can do it!*"

Whitaker chuckles. "And I mean it! But I have to tell you that my fee for this will be two hundred dollars an hour plus expenses."

"Two hundred an hour? Look, Mr. Whitaker," you say, "I only have seven cents!"

Again he chuckles. "You're a good kid—you probably have a very nice mom and dad. I'll tell you what. I'll only charge you seven cents."

For a moment you think Mr. Whitaker is being sarcastic, but the smile on his face tells you he really means it.

"Gee, thanks," you say.

Turn to page 70.

"So what are you going to do?" Cheetah asks.

"Go to the police, I guess. See if they know of anyone looking for me."

"Oh, man, I wouldn't do that. They'll call the children's shelter and Conklin will get them to send you back. He'll blame you for setting the fire chief on him and then for running away. He'll have you transferred to the reformatory." Cheetah shakes his head. "Look, you better come to Chicago with me. My brother will help you. He knows people. We can hitchhike—it's only about a six-hour drive from Center City. I'll share my bankroll with you."

"Your bankroll of ten bucks?"

"More like nine dollars and sixty cents," he says with a grin. "Anyway, someone will stake us to a meal. People will feel sorry for us."

A few miles later the bus pulls off the interstate and drives down a long boulevard before coming to a stop at the bus station.

"Center City," the driver announces.

You've got to decide what to do. The police might be looking for someone of your description. It seems foolish not to talk to them. On the other hand, the thought of being sent back to Mr. Conklin is horrible.

*If you decide to go talk to the police,
turn to page 102.*

*If you decide to stick with Cheetah,
turn to page 112.*

You wake up lying by the side of the road. Your head is pounding. It aches even more as you try to sit up and look around you. Cars are parked nearby. A police cruiser is blocking off traffic. An ambulance pulls up to a stop.

You try to remember what happened. Suddenly it comes back: you were visiting your uncle Norman. You'd had a good time there with your cousin Charlie, doing things like horseback riding and river-rafting. One day when you were walking down the road near Uncle Norman's farm a van pulled up. Some men grabbed you and kept you prisoner while they drove hundreds, maybe even a thousand miles. Most of the time they hardly talked to you. Then they realized that you weren't who they thought you were. They got very angry, not just at you but at each other. Driving along an interstate, they threw you out of their van. You landed in a ditch, and here you are now. *Except it's not the same place!* There is no ditch here. You don't remember any curve in the road like the one here. This isn't even the interstate!

"Can you talk?" A paramedic is kneeling beside you, taking your pulse.

"I think so," you say in a husky voice.

"Good, then just relax," he says. "How do you feel?"

"Bruised. Wrenched around. And I have a headache." But as you say this you're thinking that you have more than a headache. Your memory is completely mixed up.

Turn to page 38.

You start back along the track, moving as fast as you can. There's a five-foot-high wall on either side—you wouldn't want the ride to start up and have a cart coming down the track at you. But that's exactly what happens! Lights go on. The first cart barrels toward you!

There are a couple of teenage boys in it. Just as you spot them, you hear a tremendous roar. You look over your shoulder and see a *Tyrannosaurus rex* looming over you. You know it's fake and it's just there to scare people. You're more worried about the cart. It's coming at you at about thirty miles an hour, and you can't jump out of the way.

"Stop the cart!" you scream at the guys riding in it. They scream back. They can't control the cart, and even if someone hears your screams it won't make any difference. This is the Cave of Nightmares: everyone is expected to scream!

The cart is coming on as fast as ever. It's only a few feet away. Without thinking, you leap up and let the two boys catch you. It must be like catching someone falling out a window, but they manage to do it, deftly letting you down in the backseat. You get a few bruises, and they probably do too, but no one seems hurt.

The cart is headed straight toward a robot monster, but you remain perfectly calm. It doesn't even seem important to know who you are. Right now, you're just glad to be alive.

The End

He pulls an instant camera out of his desk, aims at you, and snaps the shutter. He waits a few seconds, then pulls the developed picture out of the camera and holds it up for you to see. "That's all I need from you now," he says. "Just tell me where I can reach you."

You give him Lars's name, address, and telephone number. Then you wait with Cheetah in the office for Lars to pick you up. About ten minutes later, you're still waiting when Mr. Whitaker comes out of his office.

"Someone on the phone for you," he says.

"For me?" *Who would be calling me?* you wonder. Without thinking about it, you go into his office and pick up the phone. A second later you practically jump out of your shoes. It's your mom—you recognize her voice, and who she is, and who *you* are. Just listening to her shocks your memory back.

She's extremely happy to hear your voice, and you feel the same way about hers. You realize how wonderful it is to know your own name.

Your mom says that she and your dad will fly to Chicago on the first plane they can get, and that they should arrive by dinnertime. You give them Lars's address and tell them you'll be waiting for them.

After you hang up, you ask Mr. Whitaker how he found your parents so quickly.

Turn to page 83.

72

Cheetah is disappointed when you tell him you don't want to risk the escape. He says he'll find someone else to escape with.

Apparently he doesn't succeed, because the morning after the fire drill he's still there. But then his luck changes. His half brother, who is ten years older than he is, comes to visit. Afterward, Cheetah comes up to you, grinning.

"My brother is arranging for me to get out of here," he says. "I'm going to be able to live with him in Chicago."

"That's great," you say, and you do feel happy that Cheetah has gotten a break. You just wish you would too. As it is, you feel you'll be stuck in this dump until you're grown up!

One day a few weeks after Cheetah leaves, Mr. Conklin calls you into his office.

"Every once in a while we find suitable people to be foster parents," he says. "We have a Mr. and Mrs. Sherman who went through the files of all the children here. They saw your picture and read a description of you, and they chose you as the child they would like to be foster parents to. They'll interview you before they make their final decision, but I'm sure they will like you once they've talked to you."

"I don't want foster parents," you say. "I want my real parents."

The director frowns. "I'm sure every effort has been made to find your real parents. Now it's time you went to a foster home. You don't want to stay here forever, do you?"

Turn to page 59.

The deliveryman says, "Look, Mrs. Crusoe, I've got to be going. You sure you don't want me to take this kid over to the sheriff?"

"Sheriff Dagney? I wouldn't want *my* child dumped with that man," Mrs. Crusoe says firmly.

The deliveryman chuckles. "He *is* kind of a blockhead, now that you mention it."

"We can find the kid's family," Mr. Crusoe says.

"More likely than Sheriff Dagney can," Mrs. Crusoe adds. "In the meantime we can take much better care of"—she looks at you—"this unfortunate but fine-looking child."

"Okay, then, I'll be running along," the deliveryman says. "Good luck, kid," he says to you.

As he turns to leave, you have a slight feeling of panic. The Crusoes seem very nice, and the same goes for Damon, and even their dog. Still, you don't know who these people are. Maybe you should insist on going to the sheriff's, even if some people think he's a blockhead!

*If you decide to stay with the Crusoes,
turn to page 50.*

*If you insist on being taken to the sheriff,
turn to page 40.*

You catch up with the Crusoes near Super Wheel. Mr. and Mrs. Crusoe watch as the attendant straps you and Damon into the car. The wheel cranks up a bit to move the next car down to the ground. It takes quite a while to load all the cars.

Soon music begins playing, increasing in tempo as the wheel starts to move and gathers speed. Around and around you go, faster and faster.

This is like no other Ferris wheel. When it goes up you feel as if you weigh about three hundred pounds, and when it goes down you're absolutely weightless. At the top you feel as if you'll go flying off into space; a few seconds later as if you'll be dashed to pieces on the ground. You and Damon are both securely strapped in, but you clutch the safety bar as if your life depended on it.

Faster the wheel spins. It makes you giddy, then dizzy. You can't even talk, you're just trying to survive. It can't go on much longer, you're sure of that. Yet the wheel turns faster than ever, carrying you up to the top, where you're wrenched to one side and then the other like a mouse shaken by a cat. You try to scream, but the forces are too violent. A second later you black out.

Go on to the next page.

A few moments later you come to. The tiny car you're in is tilting crazily a hundred feet in the air. The struts holding it have broken off. You're dangling by a thin strand of cable. The wheel has stopped, but the other riders are screaming, including Damon, who is seated next to you.

Turn to page 64.

The final thing that happened was that you were riding in a car with a killer and escaped by leaping out. When you landed, you hit your head again. That shock caused the memory of everything that happened *before* you landed in the ditch to come back. At the same time it blocked out your memory of everything that had happened *since*.

You often wonder what those things were, what people you met, where you went, and what happened to you during those missing days. Unfortunately you never find out.

The End

The next morning at breakfast you learn more about the Crusoes. Mr. Crusoe makes his living by building "flying" wooden birds like the one you noticed as you were coming up the drive. Mrs. Crusoe is an astrologer. She predicts what will happen to people depending on the movement of the moon, the sun, and the planets.

Damon says that in the afternoon he usually bikes down to the lake where all the kids swim. He tells you that you can also rent canoes there and go fishing.

"You can go with Damon," says Mrs. Crusoe. "As long as you come right home afterward. If the police find you wandering around, they'll put you in a children's center until your family is found. I don't think you'd like that at all!"

"Just follow our rules and you'll be happy here," Mr. Crusoe says, pointing a finger at you. "It may take a week or so before we find your real family. In the meantime would you like to learn how to make flying wooden birds?"

"It's a good thing to learn," Damon says. "Dad sells those birds for a lot of money."

"Not that much, I'm afraid," Mr. Crusoe says.

"And we're going to build a pterodactyl, a flying dinosaur," Damon adds excitedly. "Dad's going to rig a motor on it so it will *really* fly."

You glance over at Mrs. Crusoe, who has her eyes on you. "If you prefer," she says, "I'll teach you all about astrology. It's much more useful than most people realize. In fact, it might even help you find your real family."

Turn to page 98.

Then the specialists ask you to touch your nose with your index finger with your eyes closed and to stand on one foot and touch one of your knees with the toes of the opposite foot. They spend a lot of time talking among themselves in hushed voices. Finally they tell you that you've done very well on your tests.

Meanwhile you're getting more and more impatient. You don't know where home is, but you want to go there! Every time you get to talk to a new doctor or nurse you ask whether the state police has been notified about you and whether anyone is looking for a person that fits your description. Everyone you ask says, "Oh the police are looking," or "I'm sure they'll let you know the moment they've found your family."

Your third day there a woman in a white hospital jacket comes into your room. The tag on her lapel says DR. HESTOR.

"Your diagnosis is intractable amnesia," she says. "It may clear up spontaneously at some point in the future. In the meantime I'm afraid there's nothing we can do for you." She riffles through some papers on her clipboard, shaking her head, then says, "There's no point in your staying in the hospital any longer. You're being transferred to the Shelter for Unattached Children."

You can't help getting mad when you hear this. "I don't want to go there," you say. "I want someone to find my family. All they've done here is give me stupid tests!"

Turn to page 62.

The next day after lunch, Mrs. Crusoe takes Damon into town to the dentist. You decide that this would be a good time to talk to Mr. Crusoe about your feelings and maybe demand to see the police yourself.

When you go out to the barn looking for Mr. Crusoe, you're amazed to see a police car in the driveway, just as if your thinking about them had made them come! Two policemen are talking to Mr. Crusoe. You run toward them, thinking they may be giving him a report about you! One of the officers sees you coming and points at you.

"That's the kid!" He holds a photograph out so his partner can see it. The other officer glances at it, then at you. Then he pulls a gun and holds it as if he's going to aim it at Mr. Crusoe.

"Hands behind your back!" the other officer barks.

Mr. Crusoe does as he says. In a flash, the officer shackles him with handcuffs.

You run up. "What's going on?"

One of the officers puts his hand on your shoulder. He looks at you carefully. "You all right, kid? Did they hurt you?"

"Of course I'm all right," you say, wrenching away.

At that moment another police car races up the drive, followed by yet another. Mr. Crusoe stands silently, looking down at his shoes.

"You shouldn't put handcuffs on him," you tell the policeman.

Turn to page 93.

"Why did they hire that jerk?" you ask.

"He probably had a lot of fancy degrees and stuff," Cheetah says.

You sit in silence awhile, admiring the pretty farm country going by. It's kind of soothing just riding along, until you realize how hungry you are. You didn't have breakfast, and you won't be able to eat until you get to Center City. Even then you don't have money for a good meal.

"What are you planning to do once we get there?" you ask.

Cheetah chews on his lip for a moment, as if he's not sure whether he wants to talk about it. "I want to hitchhike to Chicago. I've got a half brother who lives there. His name is Lars. I'm pretty sure he'll take me in."

"Shouldn't you call him ahead of time?"

"Not till I get to Chicago. Otherwise he might just tell me to go back home."

"Why can't you go back home?"

Cheetah doesn't answer for a minute, looking out the window instead. "I don't really want to talk about it," he says after a while. "My mom died when I was real young. As for my dad—he drinks himself silly. Sometimes silly and sometimes mean. I warned him I'd run away if he didn't stop. Let's just leave it at that."

"Sure," you say. And once again you wonder what *your* family must be like.

Cheetah points at a sign ahead: CENTER CITY: TEN MILES.

"Almost there," you say.

Turn to page 67.

"Easiest case I ever had," he says. "I faxed your picture to the FBI. Their computer identified you in less than sixty seconds. They knew all about you—you were a kidnapping victim. Obviously the kidnappers got frightened and threw you out of their vehicle. That's when you landed in the ditch and bumped your head."

When your mom and dad arrive early that evening it's the happiest moment of your life. What's especially wonderful is that every bit of your memory has come back.

You stay with your parents in a comfortable hotel that night. The next morning they say they have a couple of things to do before returning home. First you all go to Mr. Whitaker's office so that your dad can thank him and pay his fee. Mr. Whitaker tells him that he said the fee would be seven cents, and that's what it is.

"Fine," your dad says. "I'll pay the seven cents and I'll add on a hundred-dollar bonus."

After leaving Mr. Whitaker's office, you all go to Lars's studio to say good-bye and to thank him and Cheetah. You and Cheetah agree to write each other, and you ask him to visit you next summer vacation. Your dad thanks Lars for his kindness. Your mom takes a fancy to his paintings. She buys a small one of a spiderweb covered with dew, glistening in the early morning sun. You bring it home, and it's been hanging in your hallway ever since.

The End

84

It's a long ride—you wish you'd brought along a book to read. For a while you look out at the farmland going by, then you doze, and later you just close your eyes and try to remember who you are.

It's about six in the evening when the truck enters Chicago. You've heard of the city, of course—a huge metropolis set on the shores of Lake Michigan. Cheetah says the lake is so big that when the wind is blowing and the surf is pounding, you'd think you were at the ocean.

The truck goes down a long avenue flanked with office buildings. Cheetah points out the Sears Tower, the tallest building in the world. Behind it you get a glimpse of Lake Michigan.

"I'll leave you off by the bus depot," the driver says. "I'm going past it anyway."

It's about six-thirty when you and Cheetah bid him good-bye and hurry into the depot. Cheetah phones his brother Lars. You wait anxiously nearby. If Lars is away, the two of you may have to sleep on a bench.

You feel better when you see Cheetah talking excitedly into the phone. He hangs up a moment later, grinning. "I spoke to Lars—he's coming to pick us up."

Go on to the next page.

"You think we can stay with him?"

"He didn't say. But once we're there, I don't think he'll throw us out."

"What does Lars do?" you ask. "Does he have a job?"

"He's an artist—paints pictures. He lives in his studio, so I have to warn you the place smells of paint."

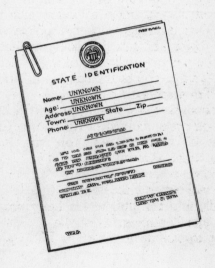

Turn to page 54.

You duck out of your room and, avoiding the elevator, race down the fire stairs. When you reach the ground floor, you walk calmly down a hallway, through the reception room, and out the main door without anyone trying to stop you. Once outside, you take off down the street, turning onto the road leading to the interstate.

It's about half a mile to the entrance ramp, so you jog along easily, pacing yourself. When you reach the ramp you stick out your thumb, trying to get a ride from the first vehicle to go by.

A gray Toyota pulls to a stop. The man at the wheel leans over and swings the passenger door open. You get in.

"Howdy," he says, flooring the accelerator. He's wearing blue jeans, sandals, and a maroon shirt open at the collar. There are a couple of large duffel bags stretched across the backseat.

"Thanks for stopping," you say.

He reaches the top of the entrance ramp and weaves into the traffic, cutting over into the fast lane. "Where are you going?"

"Ah . . . six exits down," you say, figuring that should take you far enough from Blakemore.

He nods. "I have to make a quick stop at Whitley first, a couple of exits down. I'll just be a few minutes, and then I'll take you all the way."

Turn to page 110.

"I guess I'll try the hypnotist," you tell Lars and Cheetah.

"Okay. I'll check into it," Lars says. He puts in a call and arranges for you to see the hypnotist, a Dr. Wolsey, the next morning.

Lars drives you over there after breakfast. Cheetah comes along for company. The two of them wait while Dr. Wolsey walks you down the hall to his office. He's a tiny man with a thin face and stringy white hair.

"So, I hear you've had a strange experience," he says as he shows you into his office. He asks you to sit in a straight-back chair. Then he pulls up his own chair and sets it down opposite you, only a couple of feet away. "Now tell me what happened," he says.

You tell him everything you can, which isn't much. The only thing you can remember before you found yourself in the ditch was that you were visiting your uncle Norman.

When you're finished, he says, "Your case is unusual, but not unprecedented. It's obvious that you had a very painful experience, so painful that you don't want to remember it. That would not be so bad, but the problem is that you're also blocking off your memory of everything that went on before."

"I see what you mean," you say.

"By hypnotizing you I can help you break through the barrier. Okay?"

"Sure. I hope it works," you say.

Turn to page 16.

Mrs. Crusoe continues poring over her charts, as if too deep in thought to have heard your question. Then a strange look comes over her face. "Oh my."

"What?"

"July twelfth was an inauspicious day for you to be born to us. I'm afraid we're both in great danger." Her face is drawn. The color leaves her cheeks. "A danger that could involve blood," she says gravely.

"How could this be?"

"Look." She points to a chart. "This is your constellation. That red dot is Mars, the planet of war and bloodshed. Normally another planet is nearby to temper its effect. But July twelfth . . ." She traces her fingers over the chart. "Venus, the planet of love, is directly opposite, where it has no influence at all."

She wheels around in her chair. Her face is pale, and you realize that she is truly afraid. "Evan," she says, "but I shouldn't call you that because I'm sure it's not your real name—I have to tell you something. We haven't been trying to find your parents. Damon seemed so lonely. We wanted to have you as our own child."

You leap to your feet. "That's terrible. I want to find my real family, not stay with you!"

"Of course, dear. I should have consulted my charts. Your staying here is leading to disaster. Forgive me. I'll call the state police right now. You can listen in and talk to them."

"Well, please do!" you say angrily.

Turn to page 46.

"Keep going," Reilly says.

You keep turning pages and then practically jump out of your seat. Your own picture is staring up at you! You read a description of yourself, including your name, hometown, and who your parents are—the most important things you couldn't remember! Detective Reilly cranes his neck to see what page you're on.

"I looked through this yesterday," he says, "and when you came in here I thought you looked familiar. You're not going to have to go back to the children's shelter." He takes the book from you, then picks up a telephone and starts dialing. A moment later he hands the phone to you. It's your mom!

Suddenly you remember everything about her, and everything else, too. Your whole past life comes back, as if a locked door had suddenly been opened. It's a great feeling. You know who you are, and where you live, and you know you're going home.

The End

The math teacher doesn't seem to know plus from minus. The English teacher is okay but she's usually absent. Most of the other teachers are nice enough. They just don't seem to care.

In the afternoon there are more classes plus gym, during which you play basketball inside or touch football in a small fenced-in yard outside. In the evening nearly everyone watches TV.

The kids are a mixed group. Some of them are shy and quiet. Others are loud and tough. You wonder if you'll be able to make friends with any of them. Then you realize that you're not that interested in making new friends just now— you'd rather remember the ones you had.

During your second week at the shelter you do make a friend, however—a boy with the strange name of Cheetah, like the animal. You wonder if that's his real name or just something he calls himself to sound tough. He's a thin, wiry kid who likes to arm wrestle. He must have very strong arms because he beats everyone. Cheetah has dark eyes, which dart around as if he's constantly afraid of being taken by surprise. He seems to be a loner, but he takes a liking to you —he's fascinated by how you lost your memory.

"You think you want to find your family and go home," he says. "But maybe you're like me. I ran away from home."

"You like it here better?" you ask.

"This is just as bad," he says, "but in a different way. I'd like to get out of here."

"You got any ideas how to do it?"

Turn to page 37.

The policeman turns on you. "Is that the thanks we get? We've had dozens of officers looking for you in twenty states. You didn't get hurt. You might have. Most people like him don't let their victims off so easy." He turns away and starts talking to the cops who have just arrived.

You overhear them. One of them mentions your name—your *real* name. At that moment, as if you had been hit on the head again, your memory returns. In an instant you remember who you are, where you live, and everything about yourself that you'd forgotten for so long! At the same time you realize that your suspicions were correct. The Crusoes weren't trying to find your real parents after all. They must have decided that they wanted another child, and that you would be a good one to have! It was a terribly wrong thing for them to do.

Mr. and Mrs. Crusoe must be mentally unstable, but you can't bear the thought that they might go to jail. And what would happen to Damon?

You don't have time to think about it. The policemen hustle you into one car and Mr. Crusoe into another. They tell you they are taking you both to the state police barracks, leaving the other officers to await the return of Mrs. Crusoe and Damon.

Turn to page 24.

Suddenly a boy about your own age lands on the grass twenty feet away from you! He had been up in an apple tree and you hadn't even noticed him until he jumped down from it. He has a slight build and tousled dark hair.

"Hi, my name is Damon," he says, walking toward you. "Do you live around here?"

"No, I'm just getting a ride." You motion toward the truck. You hope he doesn't ask where you're getting a ride *to*.

"Where are you getting a ride to?" Damon says.

You hesitate a moment, because you don't feel like explaining that you don't even know who you are. It turns out you don't have to say anything. The three adults are walking toward you, led by the woman. She has a triangular face and bright, gray-green eyes, very much like Damon's. She holds out her arms to you, as if she were your long-lost aunt.

You smile politely.

The woman bends down a little and looks closely into your eyes. "Is it really true—you were knocked on the head and don't know who you are?"

"It's true," you say.

The other man, heavyset with soft gray eyes, comes over. "I'm Andrew Crusoe," he says. "This is my wife Mary and my son Damon."

You glance over at Damon, who is watching awkwardly from one side.

Turn to page 73.

The car rounds a corner, and Daredevil Park comes into view. Super Wheel, billed as the biggest and fastest-moving Ferris wheel in the world, stands out against the sky. It's turning so fast you can't see much more than a blur.

"That's some wheel," you say.

"I'm not going on it," Mr. Crusoe says. "I might have a heart attack."

"Me neither," Mrs. Crusoe says. "Even if it is a safe day."

Mr. Crusoe pulls into the parking lot. He locks the car, and the four of you set off for the entrance.

"Super Wheel looks so cool," Damon says as you walk along.

"Even faster than a roller coaster," you add.

"It's already past eleven o'clock," Mr. Crusoe says when he's bought the tickets. "You kids have time to go on the Super Wheel. Then we'll have lunch at the Rain Forest Cafe."

"That's what I'm looking forward to," Mrs. Crusoe says.

Turn to page 109.

You consider whether you'd rather learn about making flying birds or about astrology. You're also thinking something else: nice as the Crusoes are, there's something a little weird about them, like this business of calling you "Evan." And the room that's all made up as if they already had another child. And their warning about what the police might do to you.

You can't help wondering if they are really trying to find your family. Maybe they want to keep you here permanently! In that case you could say you'd like a day to rest up and think about what to do. Then, when the others are busy, you could run away.

Bu maybe you're worrying needlessly.

If you decide to learn how to make flying wooden birds, turn to page 115.

If you decide to learn about astrology, turn to page 22.

If you tell the Crusoes you'd like a day to rest up and think about things, turn to page 58.

"I'm Carol Langley, from the Department of Welfare," she says. "You should be particularly interested in this. Mr. Conklin has been dismissed as director of the shelter for violation of important regulations. One of Mr. Conklin's mistakes was that he only assumed that the police were aware of your case. He never bothered to check or make any inquiries. When we found this out, we immediately notified the police and the FBI and faxed your picture to them. I'm happy to tell you that it matches the description of a missing child in their files, one they believe was kidnapped. Your parents are being notified at this very minute." She grins broadly. "You're going to be out of here in no time!"

The End

You take off, darting around the cafe, and then head for the park exit. As far as you can tell, the Crusoes didn't see where you went. But you've got another problem. A security guard is chasing you, yelling for you to stop, and he's gaining on you.

You turn sharply around a building and pass the entrance to a tunnel. Dim lights above it spell out CAVE OF NIGHTMARES. There's a chain across the entrance. A sign hanging from it says CLOSED.

Turn to page 18.

"Thanks for the invitation," you tell Cheetah as the two of you get off the bus, "but I think I'd better go to the police. It's my best chance of finding my family."

"Okay," he says. "You've been a real pal." He takes out a pencil, writes something on a scrap of paper, and hands it to you. "This is my brother's address. Write me and let me know if you ever find out who you are."

"You bet. Good luck, Cheetah."

The two of you part. You look around the bus station and spot a policeman near the main entrance. You tell him that you can't remember who you are, but you think your parents are looking for you. He calls a squad car that picks you up and brings you to headquarters.

An officer leads you to the office of the chief detective. The sign on his desk says P. J. REILLY. You don't tell him how you escaped from the children's shelter, just that you've lost your memory and need help finding out who you are.

He nods. Then he says, "Did you happen to come here from Blakemore?"

A shudder goes through you as you realize that Mr. Conklin must have put out an alarm for you.

Go on to the next page.

"Ran away from the children's shelter there?" You swallow hard. He knows, all right.

"That may not be too important," Reilly says with a grin. "Take a look through these." He hands you a loose-leaf binder. You start turning the pages. Each one has a picture of someone— many of them kids—and a typewritten description.

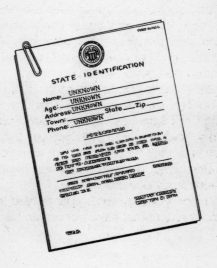

Turn to page 90.

In the distance you hear a yell from Mr. Conklin. Cheetah, running a little ahead of you, waves for you to follow as he turns down a side street. You stay close behind him.

A bus is parked at the end of the next block. Cheetah slows up.

"That's the bus to Center City," he says between breaths. "It leaves in about three minutes."

"How do you know about this?" you say.

"From the janitor."

The two of you buy tickets from the driver, forking over six dollars each.

The bus is only a third full. You and Cheetah take seats in the back and hunch down. You don't want to be spotted through the window.

"*Come on,*" Cheetah mutters. "Get this show on the road."

Turn to page 116.

You decide not to take a chance on jumping out. The driver swerves around the truck, barely avoiding an accident. Then he accelerates down the road. You shriek for him to stop. He speeds up even more, then passes another car on a curve. You hear a police siren somewhere behind you. The driver makes another screeching, skidding turn down a side road. Through the rearview mirror you see a police car speeding by. The officer must have rounded the curve seconds too late to see your car turn.

Again the driver turns sharply, hardly slowing at all. This time he's headed up a dirt road leading into the woods. You shudder as you realize that you're no longer on the public road.

Your fear is his amusement. He starts laughing and keeps laughing until he slams on the brakes, stopping the car in front of a rude stone house. You try to get out of the car, but he clutches your arm.

"Victim number twenty-two," he says.

The End

"You've really been through something!" the man says. "And you were very brave. We're all thankful you're back on the ground. What's your name?"

"I don't know," you blurt out.

"You don't know?" The man seems even more shocked than you are. But he keeps asking questions. You tell him everything that's happened to you since you found yourself lying in a ditch.

The reporter decides he has a bigger news story than he'd thought. He interviews the Crusoes, who admit that they liked having you in their family so much that they delayed trying to find out who you were!

That night the newsman's interview with you is on television across the nation. Your parents are among the millions watching. They quickly track you down and reach you by phone at the Crusoes' house. As soon as you hear your mom's voice and she says your name, your whole memory comes back—as if she'd turned a key in a lock and opened a door.

The next day your parents come to pick you up. It's a very happy moment. But they—and the police—are concerned that the Crusoes didn't notify the authorities when you first arrived at their house.

Turn to page 39.

"Fire! Fire!" someone shouts. A bunch of kids run toward you. Suddenly they are pressing in around you, angry they can't get out.

"It's locked!" Cheetah yells. But the kids don't seem to believe him.

"Come on!" You grab Cheetah's arm. The two of you try to break your way through the mob of kids pushing you, but they're panicked, blocking your way.

A voice shouts over the screams and clanging bells. "Go the other way!" It's Mr. Conklin, standing in the hallway. He is almost knocked over as the kids who were pressing against you follow his order.

"Cheetah, can we get to the tree from the other exit?" you ask.

"No way," he says. "Only from here."

Suddenly someone—you see it's Mr. Conklin —grips you.

"Come on, you two. I said to exit through the other door!" You and Cheetah rush past him and follow the crowd out the other door. The night proctor makes you all line up in the yard.

A minute later two fire trucks and a police car come racing up. The night proctor opens the iron gate, and a couple of firemen come through it, searchlights and pickaxes in hand. Other firemen start uncoiling a fire hose.

"All you kids stay here," Mr. Conklin barks. He goes out to talk to the fire chief and sends the night proctor back to check on the building.

Turn to page 35.

Inside the park, Damon races toward the Super Wheel. His parents hurry to keep up. You hang back a little, passing the Rain Forest Cafe. You could dart around it and be out of sight in a few seconds. On the other hand, the Crusoes have been pretty nice to you. Maybe you should stick with them.

*If you decide to take off,
turn to page 100.*

*If you decide to stay with the Crusoes,
turn to page 74.*

110

"All right," you say, but you don't feel very comfortable about it. There's something odd about his tone of voice. You wonder if it was a good idea to hitchhike.

He speeds along, passing every car in sight.

"Well," the man says. "Isn't it a nice day?"

"Yes," you say.

He glances over at you. "Yet even though it's a nice day, some people are having a bad day—a very bad day. Isn't that sad?"

"Yes it is." Now you're *sure* you shouldn't have hitchhiked!

He glances over at you again. "That's the way it works," he says. "Some people have to have a bad day. For some, it's the last day they'll ever have."

"I guess so," you say. By now you're desperately trying to plan what to do.

He gives you a long look.

"Say, I think I better get out," you say. "Please pull over."

"Not here," he says. "It would be dangerous to stop here."

You glance at the door, looking for the latch. He's going to have to slow down when he comes off the interstate. That's when you could bail out. You study just how your hand will have to move to get the door open fast.

Go on to the next page.

The man drives on, racing through traffic until he's out in the clear with no other cars around. From time to time he makes more weird comments about death and dying. You try not to let on that you're suspicious, even though you're more than suspicious: you're convinced he's a psycho!

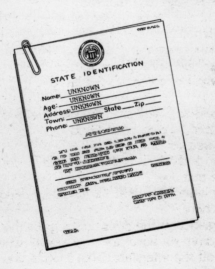

Turn to page 63.

"I'll stick with you, Cheetah," you say as the two of you get off the bus.

"I hoped you would," he says.

You walk through the bus station together. "Look," you say. "There's a map of Center City —on that wall."

"C'mon," Cheetah says. The two of you go over to the map. An arrow on it, pointing to the bus station, says YOU ARE HERE.

Cheetah traces his finger across the map. "That's what we want, the entrance to the interstate, northbound. That will take us to Chicago."

"It's dangerous to hitchhike," you say.

Cheetah shrugs. "Not that dangerous. Besides, what else are we going to do?"

"And the cops may pick us up before we get a ride," you say.

"So, you were thinking of going to the police anyway," he says. "Look, it's a risk, but I'm taking it."

"The interstate entrance looks about half a mile from here," you say. "We can walk, but let's get something to eat first."

Go on to the next page.

"Right, but not here. We'll get more for our money at a supermarket. Come on. I still have moolah."

Cheetah and you stock up on soda, corn chips, and a couple of apples, spending all but the last dollar-fifty of Cheetah's money. Then you set out for the highway. You reach the ramp leading onto the interstate about mid-day. Almost immediately a tractor-trailer pulls to a stop.

Turn to page 32.

You decide to learn how to make flying wooden birds. The next morning you and Damon join Mr. Crusoe in his workshop in the barn. He shows you how he draws the outline of the body of the bird, its wings and head, then traces them onto wood and cuts out the shapes. Then he shows you how he assembles the pivots and springs that make the wings flap. Once the bird is ready to "fly," imitation feathers are carved in the wood. It is further shaped and decorated and then painted or varnished.

Mr. Crusoe says he's trying to make certain that you and Damon understand how everything is done so that you can design and make flying birds yourselves. You can see it will take a while. You'll have to become a designer, a carpenter, and a mechanic all at once!

From then on you and Damon spend your mornings in the workshop. After a few weeks, you finish making your first bird. It's an exciting moment. You can't wait to take it home and show it to your parents!

What parents? You suddenly realize how long you've been with the Crusoes without their being able to find your real family. Again you become suspicious that they are not really trying. If Mr. Crusoe had called the police or the missing persons bureau, wouldn't they have sent someone to talk to you? No one's even *tried* to make you remember who you are!

Turn to page 81.

A man comes rushing up to the bus. For a second you think he's after you, but he's just a passenger afraid he'd miss the bus. He pays his fare, and once he's seated, the driver starts up.

You sigh with relief as the bus pulls away, but that feeling doesn't last long. You and Cheetah will soon be in a strange city with almost no money in your pockets. And you still have no memory of who you are. What will you do? What future is there for you?

Riding along in the bus, you and Cheetah talk about the children's shelter and how glad you are to get away from it. "The whole trouble is that guy Conklin," Cheetah says. "If they had a decent person running the place, it would help kids instead of turning them sour."

Turn to page 82.

The next day you see a headline in the paper that reads: PSYCHOPATHIC KILLER APPREHENDED AFTER INTENDED VICTIM JUMPS FROM CAR. There's a picture of you, the "intended victim," and a picture of the killer. You don't precisely remember having seen him before, but somehow he looks familiar.

In the days ahead you come to realize the shocking truth: you were kidnapped near your uncle Norman's farm and thrown in the ditch just as you remembered. Then a lot of things happened to you because you had lost your memory when you landed in the ditch!

Turn to page 76.

118

The van driver takes you inside and turns you over to the director, Mr. Conklin, a small, slightly stooped man with a hooked nose. Thin, wispy strands of hair are slicked down over his almost bald head. He introduces himself and asks you to step inside his office. You sit across from his desk while he flips through a stack of papers. He stops to read something.

"Well," he says without looking up, "your file indicates that you're an unusual case. Intractable amnesia. Too bad, too bad."

"What does my file show about the police trying to find my family?" you ask.

"Why they're looking, of course."

"I'm surprised the police haven't come to interview me," you say.

He gives you a severe look. "Well, why should they? You've told everyone you can't remember anything."

Turn to page 8.

The Crusoes tell you how happy they are that you've got your memory back. Then Mrs. Crusoe insists on knowing what your real date of birth is. When you tell her, she rushes to her desk and begins studying her charts.

A moment later the phone rings. It's your parents. They are overjoyed to hear your voice and say they're coming to pick you up. The police have arranged for you to be driven to the airport where they'll be arriving.

When you hang up, Mrs. Crusoe comes up to you, a big smile on her face. "It's just wonderful," she says.

"That I got my memory back?"

"Of course *that's* wonderful," she says. "But I'm thinking of the stars you were born under, the position of the planets the day you were born. The celestial conjunctions are perfect! Despite the bad experience you've had, you're going to have a most wonderful life. It's written in the stars!"

The End

ABOUT THE AUTHOR

EDWARD PACKARD is a graduate of Princeton University and Columbia Law School. He developed the unique storytelling approach used in the Choose Your Own Adventure series while thinking up stories for his children, Caroline, Andrea, and Wells.

ABOUT THE ILLUSTRATOR

FRANK BOLLE studied at Pratt Institute. He has worked as an illustrator for many national magazines and now creates and draws cartoons for magazines as well. He has also worked in advertising and children's educational materials and has drawn strips, including *Annie* and *Winnie Winkle*. He has illustrated many books in the Choose Your Own Adventure series, including *Master of Kung Fu, Return of the Ninja, Through the Black Hole, The Worst Day of Your Life, Master of Tae Kwon Do, The Cobra Connection, Hijacked!, Master of Karate, Invaders from Within, The Lost Ninja, Daredevil Park, Kidnapped!, Master of Martial Arts,* and *Master of Judo.* A native of Brooklyn Heights, New York, Mr. Bolle now lives and works in Westport, Connecticut.